BAD KITTY

Does NOT Like SNOW

NICK BRUEL

A NEAL PORTER BOOK
ROARING BROOK PRESS
New York

It is snowing.

Kitty has never seen snow.

Kitty does not know
what snow is.

So Kitty asks the computer,

The computer tells Kitty . . .
Snow is cold.
Snow is wet.
Snow is slippery.
Snow is soft.

Now Kitty is ready for the snow.

The snow is cold.

The snow is wet.

The snow is slippery.

The snow is soft.

The computer is wrong.

Snow is **VERY** soft!
Snow is **VERY** slippery!
Snow is **VERY** wet!

And snow is VERY, VERY, VERY, COLD!

Kitty does not like computers.

Kitty does not like snow.